P9-DHN-182

PILLS

IDEAL

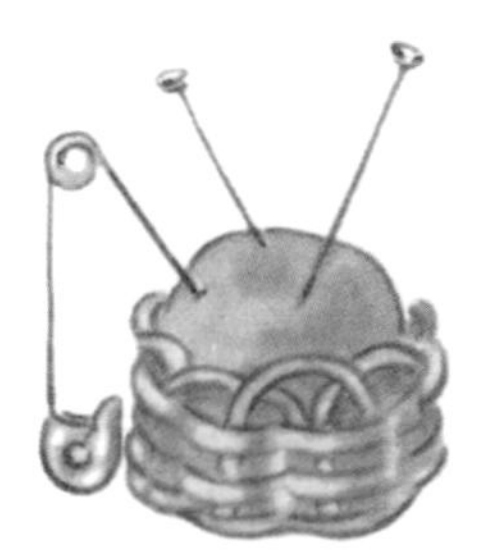

GLUE

—BIG SUSAN—

BIG SUSAN

55th ANNIVERSARY EDITION

by

ELIZABETH ORTON JONES

TEXAS • PURPLE HOUSE PRESS • 2002

Published by
Purple House Press
1625 Village Trail
Keller, TX 76248
www.PurpleHousePress.com

Library of Congress Cataloging-in-Publication Data
Jones, Elizabeth Orton, 1910-
Big Susan / written and illustrated by Elizabeth Orton Jones — 1st ed.
p. cm.
Previously published: New York : Macmillan, 1947
Summary: After six weeks of neglect, a family of dolls comes to life on Christmas Eve wondering if they will have a tree or gifts this year from a girl who normally takes such good care of them.
ISBN: 1-930900-06-6 (hardcover : alk. paper)
[1. Dolls – Fiction 2. Christmas – Fiction] I. Title.
PZ7.J69 Bi 2002 Fic - dc21 2002003656

Printed in South Korea
1 2 3 4 5 6 7 8 9 10
First Edition

To my own Mr. and Mrs. Doll
this book is faithfully
dedicated

Contents

One Morning

One morning Mr. and Mrs. Doll got out of bed and came downstairs. They didn't have to stop to dress, for they always slept with their clothes on.

Mr. Doll sat down at the table in the dining room. Mrs. Doll sat down at the piano in the living room. They sat very stiffly, for they were made of celluloid and could not bend.

Mrs. Doll opened the piano. It had six white keys and three black. "Shall I play something for you, dear, while you eat your breakfast?" she called. Mrs. Doll could play one piece on the piano. It was called "Chopsticks."

"Thank you, dear, that would be very nice," Mr. Doll called back. " 'Music calms the nerves,' they say. My nerves are always rather jumpy in the morning!"

So Mrs. Doll began to play.

The old china Cook, who had loose joints and was very wobbly, brought the plaster coffee cake in from the kitchen, dropping it twice on the way. But at last she managed to get it to the dining room table and to set it down before Mr. Doll. Mr. Doll always had the plaster coffee cake for his breakfast.

The Cook wobbled back to the kitchen. Mr. Doll sat stiffly, enjoying his coffee cake and listening to "Chopsticks," which Mrs. Doll kept playing for him over and over. He was about to call to Mrs. Doll to say that her playing sounded quite lovely today, when—

Suddenly Mr. Doll found that he could neither speak nor move.

Mrs. Doll stopped playing.

The Cook in the kitchen fell—plunk!—to the floor.

Upstairs in the nursery Mr. and Mrs. Doll's six celluloid children stayed right where they were, asleep on their bed.

But the celluloid Nurse, who was in the bathroom washing her face at that moment, suddenly found herself standing on her head in the basin with her feet sticking straight up in the air!

Now the dolls were quite used to this sort of thing. It happened every day. But it never lasted very long. It happened whenever Susan had other things to think about—whenever Susan had other things to do.

Who was Susan?

Susan was the Wonderful Person to whom the Dolls belonged. She was so big they had never seen all of her—that is, not all of her at one time. Once in a while they saw her whole face. But usually it was only part of her face and one or the other of her taffy-colored pigtails. Susan's hands were what they saw most often.

There was no front to the Doll house. Susan could reach right in and move things about. With one of her hands she could pick up three children at once, or both Mr. and Mrs. Doll together. But they were not a bit afraid, for Susan was very gentle. She never dropped anybody. Susan could lift a whole bed with six children asleep in it right out of the house and put it back without even waking them, so gentle was she.

Her face was not a bit like celluloid, nor like china. It was soft and warm and alive. And sometimes it smelled of soap and water, and sometimes it smelled of cinnamon toast. And sometimes, especially at night, it smelled sweetly and faintly of tooth paste. And that was the Doll children's most favorite smell in the world.

Susan would often peep into the nursery at night, when the children were in bed, to make sure they were nicely covered, as children should be. They could not see her face at all, then, because it was dark; but they knew she was near, for their favorite smell was in the air—the sweet, faint, good-night smell of Susan's tooth paste.

The Dolls could neither speak nor move when Susan was not there. Nor could they walk without her help—nor eat, nor drink, nor go to bed, nor get up; nor could any housekeeping be done, for this, too, depended upon Susan.

They were used to Susan's hands reaching in to help them. They knew whenever they spoke that it was really Susan speaking for them. They understood how this was a part of being what they were. And they didn't mind a bit, for they loved Susan.

There was, of course, one short night in every year when they needed no help from Susan—the Night between twelve o'clock of Christmas Eve and the dawn of Christmas Morning—that Wonderful Night when all dolls come alive and can speak. But once a year is not very often.

The rest of the time they depended upon Susan.

When they were sick, Susan took care of them. When they wanted something very much, they had only to ask and Susan would give it to them—that is, if it were not too silly.

Once Freddie Doll had asked and asked for a wrist watch. But he never got it.

"What a silly thing to ask for, Freddie!" his mother had said, though he knew it was really Susan speaking. "You are much too

small for a wrist watch. Besides, there are two perfectly good clocks in the house: the one in the living room that says *quarter before seven,* and Cook's alarm clock that says *quarter past eleven.* You must learn to ask for sensible things!"

It was a different matter when, one night, Mr. and Mrs. Doll had asked for a new baby. Susan had begun saving her pennies at once. But it was going to be quite some time before she could buy the beautiful china baby she had in mind for Mr. and Mrs. Doll. Christmas was only seven weeks away. There were other presents to buy. And there were *many* other things to think about—*many* other things to do.

The Wonderful Night

Mr. Doll was still sitting at breakfast in the dining room. The dishes were all dusty. The plaster coffee cake had fallen to the floor and rolled beneath the table. A long cobweb hung from the ceiling.

Six whole weeks had gone by.

"Ah me!" thought Mr. Doll, still not able to speak or move. "This is getting rather tiresome!"

Mrs. Doll was still sitting at the piano in the living room. On top of the piano lay the carpet sweeper.

"Mercy!" thought Mrs. Doll, staring at the carpet sweeper. "Now just look at that! Why, this living room is a disgrace!"

Indeed it was.

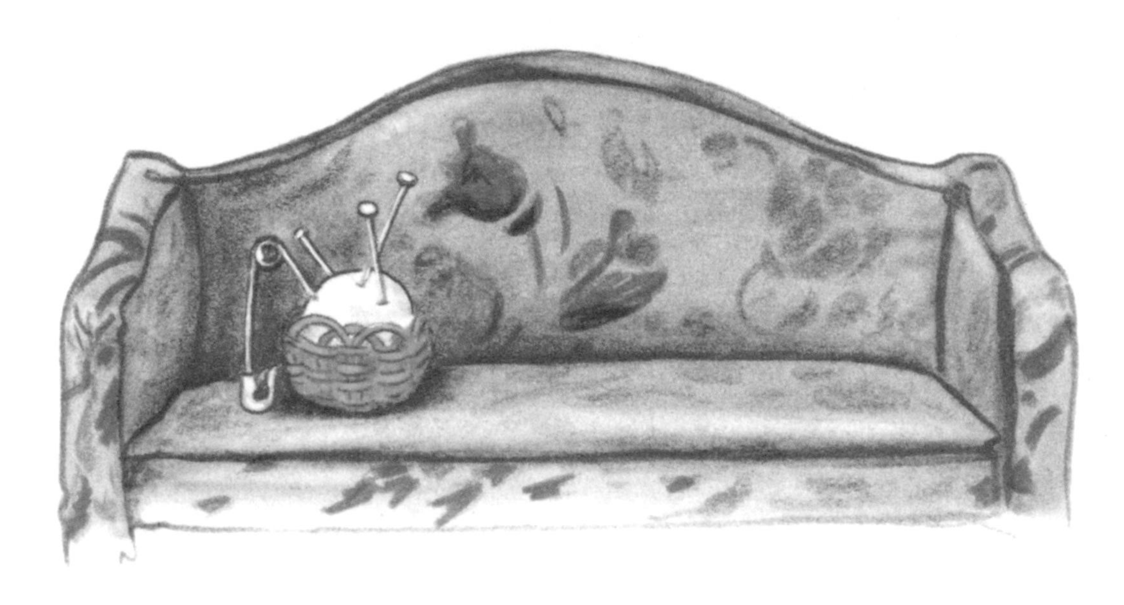

Mrs. Doll's pincushion was on the sofa. The best yellow silk sofa pillow was in the fireplace. Mr. Doll's ash stand had tipped over; his one and only cigar had rolled out onto the rug. On top of the clock on the mantelpiece was the Cook's wig.

The Cook was still lying on the floor in the kitchen. On the floor around her were pots and pans, knives and forks, some jacks, and the golf tee which served as the Dolls' potato masher. On the stove stood a lamp with a green shade.

"Ach!" thought the Cook. "Six weeks it is now! And where's the end to it? Where's the end?"

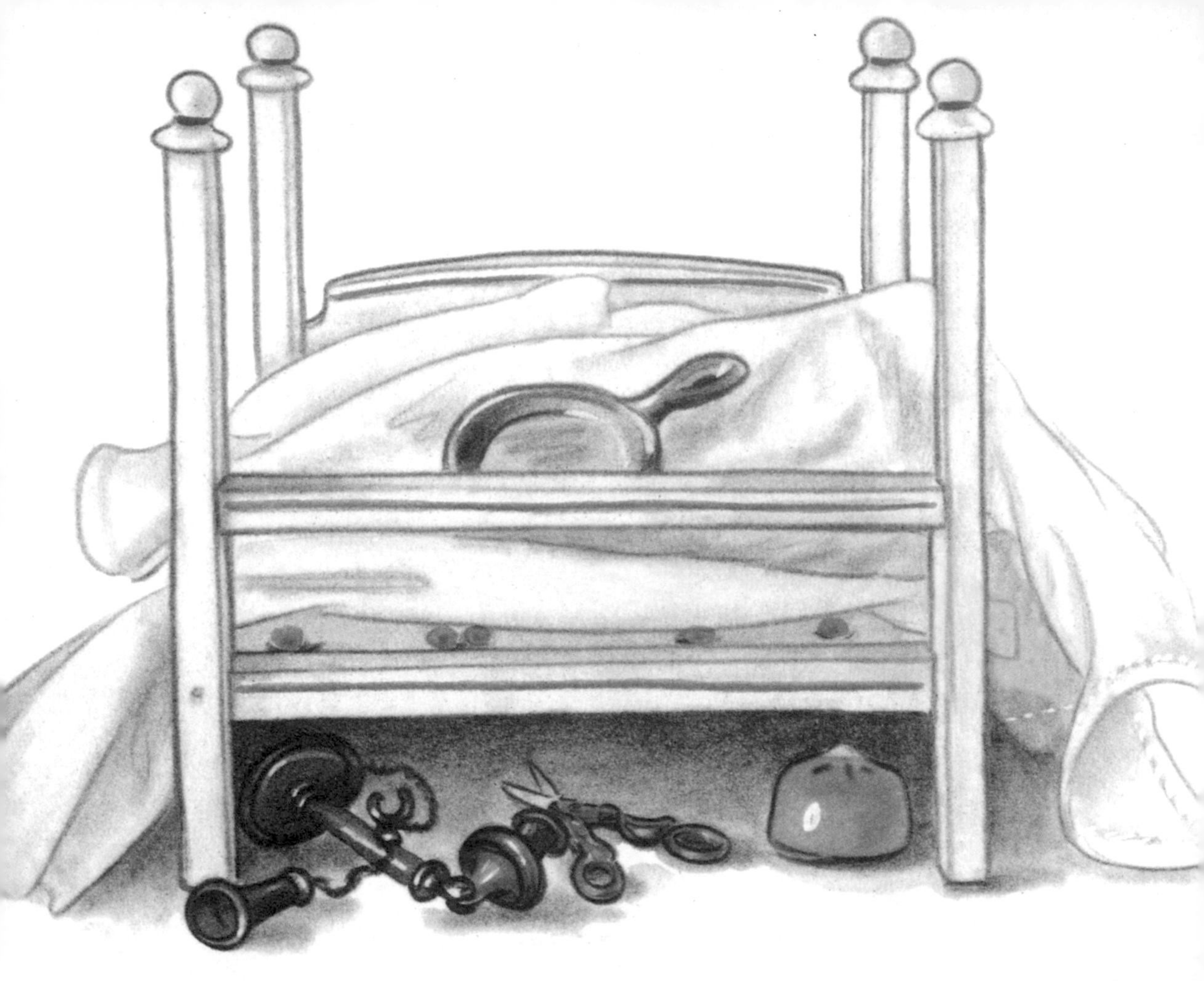

Upstairs, in Mr. and Mrs. Doll's room, the bed was still unmade. In the middle of the bed lay a frying pan. On Mrs. Doll's dainty white dresser lay the logs that belonged in the fireplace. Mrs. Doll's sewing basket had tipped over. Her scissors were under the bed. So were the telephone and a pink plaster pudding with a rosebud on top. The pudding was *frightfully* dusty.

On the bed in the nursery lay Mr. and Mrs. Doll's six celluloid children, in a heap.

On the floor were three jacks, a big elastic garter, a big button, and a bright green marble.

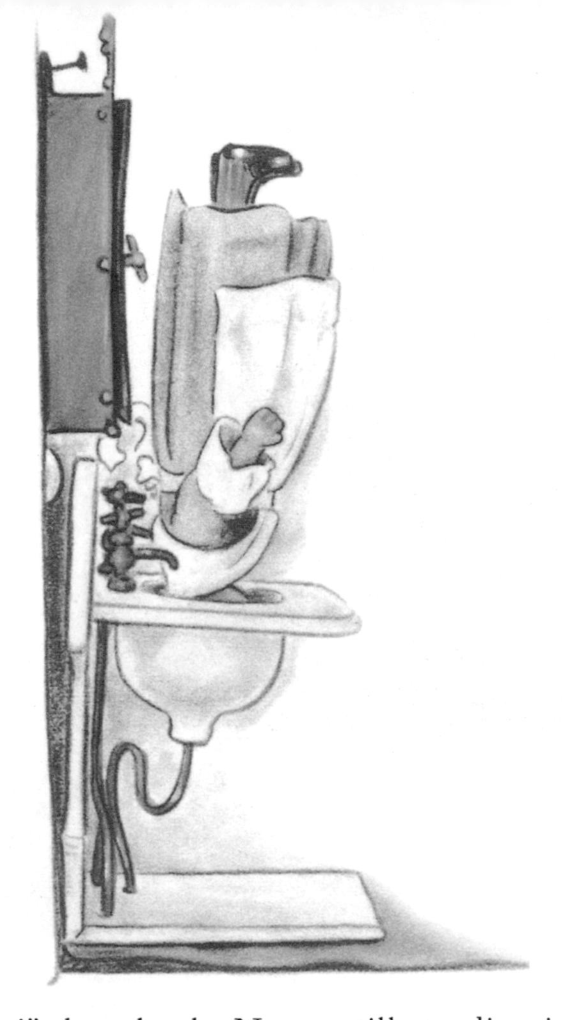

"Dear sakes!" thought the Nurse, still standing in the basin in the bathroom on her head. "Six weeks!"

Also in the bathroom stood the ironing board, though there was scarcely room for it. On it lay Mr. Doll's ax. A large wooden egg with a purple pansy painted on it was in the bathtub; *Easter Greetings,* it said—rather out of season!

In the little room up over the kitchen where the Cook slept was a piece of white cardboard. To the cardboard was fastened a brand-new china baby with pink cheeks and a long white dress and a tiny lace bonnet with pink bows. This was the baby Mr. and Mrs. Doll had asked for, so long ago. But they hadn't seen it yet. They didn't even know it was in the house.

No one knew except Susan.

But *where was she?*

Day after day had gone by—and no Susan. Six whole weeks had gone by—and still no Susan. Why, she hadn't even peeped into the nursery at night to make sure the children were nicely covered, as children should be!

Where *was* she?

Six more days and six more nights went by; and they were all alike to the Dolls, who could neither speak nor move.

But at last there came one Night which was not like any other.

Late it was, and very dark, when Mr. Doll heard the tinkle-tinkle of the piano in the living room, and someone softly singing:

"Away in a manger..."

Mr. Doll thought he had never in all his life heard anything so lovely. He rose from the table, felt his way across the dining room in the dark, and stood in the doorway listening:

"No crib for His bed..."

"Dear?" whispered Mr. Doll.

"Yes, dear?" answered Mrs. Doll.

"Is that *you* singing?"

"Yes, dear."

"I'd forgotten you could sing!" whispered Mr. Doll. "I'd forgotten you could play anything but 'Chopsticks'! Please go on—"

So Mrs. Doll went on singing:

"The little Lord Jesus
Lay down His sweet head."

"Why!" thought Mr. Doll. "It must be Christmas Eve!"

Of course! But it had come in such a quiet way, this year, that Mr. Doll had not even noticed. Why, he had come alive! He could speak! He could move! He could *bend*!

He felt his way over to Mrs. Doll and bent down and kissed her.

"At last!" she whispered. "The Wonderful Night is here!" Then, out loud, she said, "Do let's have some light, dear!"

Mr. Doll felt his way over to the little button which was glued to the wall, and pushed it, and there was light everywhere in the house. It was not electric—it was pretend-light, a kind that costs nothing and never gets out of order.

There were noises upstairs in the nursery—the noises of six excited children who had come alive, too.

"Look!" shouted Freddie, bending over and touching the floor. "Look what I can do!"

"Look what *I* can do!" laughed George, turning a somersault.

"Look at *me*!" shouted Mary, doing a backbend.

"That's nothing!" laughed Jane, and she turned a cartwheel across the nursery.

Something for Susan

"Say, dear—" said Mrs. Doll, pointing to the top of the piano, "would you reach up and get down that carpet sweeper? I can't bear to see it there another minute!"

As Mr. Doll reached up, there were noises on the stairs. And the very next moment the children came into the living room—shouting, laughing, jumping, bending, hugging their father and mother, and hugging one another.

Then, suddenly, they stopped still, staring.

"Where's the Christmas tree?" asked Tommy. "Isn't there any Christmas tree?"

"Where are all the presents?" asked Ann.

"I want a wrist watch!" said Freddie.

"Children, children—" said Mrs. Doll, getting up from the piano bench.

She pulled the yellow silk sofa pillow out of the fireplace, and shook it. She stood up Mr. Doll's ash stand. She took the pincushion from the sofa and handed it to Jane. Then she sat down on the sofa, with the yellow silk pillow behind her, and burst into tears.

"Mother!" said the children, scrambling onto the sofa beside her. "Why are you crying?"

"I'm afraid, children," said Mrs. Doll, taking out her handkerchief, "there'll be no tree—nor presents—this year!"

"Now, now, dear!" said Mr. Doll, reaching over and patting her on the shoulder. "We'll fix up something. We'll do something! We can't have *tears* on *Christmas*!"

"We can't have presents, either—without Susan!" said Mrs. Doll, drying her eyes with her handkerchief. "Presents mean so much to the children! And we've always had a tree! Susan used to stand it—right there!" Mrs. Doll pointed with her handkerchief to the middle of the rug. "She would always trim the tree and put presents all around it before she went to bed. Remember? And there everything would be, ready for us at midnight. But this year—*this* year—it looks as if—Susan had forgotten us!" Again Mrs. Doll burst into tears.

The children sat still as six little mice, staring at their mother. Why! Their mother had always told them that Susan would never forget! *Never!* No matter what!

Mr. Doll reached down and picked up his one and only cigar from the rug. "Well, now—" he said, twiddling the cigar with his fingers, "why don't we just decide that this is going to be a different sort of Christmas? There's more to Christmas than presents, you know, and more to Christmas than Susan."

"Why, dear!" said Mrs. Doll. Then she said, "Well—yes—that's true."

Mr. Doll sat down in the easy chair with his cigar. "Christmas is a big thing—" he said, "a very big thing. It takes in the whole world and leaves nobody out... Look at us, for instance! What are we?"

The children stared at their father.

"Little celluloid dolls—that's all we are," said their father. "And yet—look at what has happened to us tonight! Why, we've come alive! Isn't that wonderful? Isn't that enough? Do we need presents, too?"

"But presents are fun!" said the children.

"There are other kinds of fun," said Mr. Doll. "Just sitting quietly, like this, and talking together, is one kind."

"But it's Christmas!" said the children, jumping up. "We want presents!"

"I want a wrist watch!" said Freddie.

"All right—" said Mr. Doll. "Suppose I decide to give Freddie a wrist watch."

"What!" said Freddie, running to the easy chair and hugging his father.

"I said—*suppose*!" laughed his father. "Just—suppose!... All right—who would buy the wrist watch?"

"Susan—" said Freddie, sitting down on the rug.

"Who would wrap it in tissue paper and tie it with string and write *For Freddie* on the little label?"

"Susan—" said the rest of the children, sitting down beside Freddie on the rug.

"All right—" said Mr. Doll. "But, now, suppose—"

"Say, I have an idea!" said Mrs. Doll, suddenly, putting away her handkerchief.

"Susan has always done everything for us," said Mrs. Doll. "*This* year—why don't *we* do something for *Susan*?"

"What could *we* do?" asked the children. "We're so little—and Susan's so big!"

Mrs. Doll looked up at the living room ceiling. She saw several cobwebs hanging there. "We could clean this house from top to bottom!" she said. "We could put it all in order!"

"Now, dear!" said Mr. Doll. "Couldn't we think of something better to do for Susan? Why, that's no kind of a—why, that's—nothing!"

"Nothing?" said Mrs. Doll, getting up from the sofa. "Just you wait till we begin!"

"No, really! Do you think Susan would *like* that?" asked Mr. Doll. He did not think much of cleaning house.

"She'd like it better than anything, I'm sure," said Mrs. Doll, looking at the clock. "Now, let's see. If we begin right away, I think we can be through by morning! Oh, won't Susan be surprised!"

"Won't Susan be surprised! Won't Susan be *surprised*!" sang the children, clapping their hands and jumping up from the rug.

"Ah me!" sighed Mr. Doll, laying down his cigar. "Well? Where do we begin?"

His question was answered by a voice from the kitchen. "Mr. Doll! Ach! Mrs. Doll! Help!" It was the voice of the Cook.

A Different Sort of Christmas

Mr. and Mrs. Doll and the children went running through the dining room to the kitchen. And there on the floor, with pots and pans and knives and forks all around her, sat the Cook, holding her head.

"Ach! My *wig*! My beauti-ful wig! It's *gone*!" she said. "Where is it?"

"I know where it is!" said Tommy. And back to the living room he ran, to get it from the top of the clock.

"Jane, hurry and get me the glue and some bandages!" said Mrs. Doll, pushing a couple of pots aside with her foot. She leaned down and dusted out the inside of the Cook's head, very carefully, with her handerkerchief.

"Don't worry, Cook!" said Mr. Doll, watching. "We'll fix it!"

LUX
HEINZ

Jane hurried upstairs to the bathroom for the glue and the bandages, which were in the medicine chest.

"Eek!" she screamed as she got there. "Father! Come quick!"

Mr. Doll ran up, two steps at a time, to the bathroom. And there, still standing on her head in the basin, was the Nurse. "Gracious!" said Mr. Doll. "Are you all right, Nurse?"

"Of course I'm all right!" said the Nurse. "But I'd just like to say here and now that seven weeks in this position is just about enough!"

"Nurse!" laughed Jane. "It's Christmas! You can get down from there! You can bend! We all can!"

"Nonsense!" said the Nurse.

"Try it!" said Mr. Doll. "Just bend—and down you'll come. Jane and I are right here to catch you."

The Nurse bent her knees, pushed against the medicine chest with her feet, and—sure enough—down she came. "Well, I declare!" she said, straightening her apron.

Jane stood on tiptoe and opened the medicine chest. She took out the glue and the roll of bandages; and also the adhesive plaster, a safety pin, and the bottle of pills, in case they should be needed. Then she and her father and the Nurse carried these things downstairs to the kitchen.

"Thanks!... Oh! Merry Christmas, Nurse!" said Mrs. Doll, shaking out the Cook's wig, which Tommy had brought.

"Merry Christmas to you, Mrs. Doll!" said the Nurse, staring down into the Cook's head.

Mrs. Doll smeared glue all around the outside of the Cook's head. Then she smeared glue inside the wig. Then, after making sure which was the back and which was the front, she set the wig in place.

The Cook reached up and turned it a little this way—a little that way—until it felt just right. Then Mrs. Doll wound a bandage around and around, over the wig and under the Cook's chin, and fastened it with adhesive plaster and the safety pin.

"There!" said Mrs. Doll.

"Thank you kindly, ma'am!" said the Cook as Mr. Doll helped her to her feet. "I expect *I'm* a sight to see!"

"You look all right," said Mr. Doll. "How do you feel?"

"Still a bit wobbly, sir," said the Cook.

"I'd say she needed a pill, Mrs. Doll," said the Nurse. "There's nothing like a pill to pep a person up!"

Mrs. Doll opened the bottle and gave the Cook a couple of pills. They were not *real* pills. They were birthday-cake candy. They tasted very good.

Mr. Doll took the Cook's arm, led her into the living room, and seated her in the easy chair.

"Ain't *I* the grand lady, though!" she said as Mr. Doll brought the green velvet footstool for her feet.

"Now just take it easy, Cook, till your glue is dry. Here—" said Mr. Doll, handing her a book.

"Ach! Thank you kindly, sir!" said the Cook, taking it and opening it and trying to look as if she were really enjoying it. She did not know how to read.

Mr. Doll went back to the kitchen, where Mrs. Doll was filling a pail with water, at the sink. It was only pretend-water. But that is better than no water at all. The pail was a large-sized thimble.

Jane was putting away the pots and pans and knives and forks which had been on the floor.

Ann was dusting the plaster coffee cake, which Mary had brought from the dining room.

"Where does *this* go?" asked Freddie, meaning the lamp with the green shade.

"In the living room—on top of the piano," said Mrs. Doll. "Say, dear—will you get me the scrubbing brush? I think I saw it in the oven."

"What in the world is *this*?" asked Tommy, meaning a jack.

"I'm sure I don't know," said Mrs. Doll, setting the pail of pretend-water down on the floor. "Where did you find it?"

"Right here," said Tommy.

"Here's another just like it!" said George, pulling another jack from under the table. "What *are* they?"

Mr. Doll, who had found the scrubbing brush, studied the two jacks. "I never saw such crazy-looking things!" he said. "What are they for?"

"Can *we* have them, Mother?" asked Tommy. "For toys?"

"Do anything you like with them," said Mrs. Doll as Mr. Doll handed her the scrubbing brush, "only take them away from here!"

"Mrs. Doll—" said the Nurse, coming in from the dining room with her arms full of dusty dishes, "I don't know if I'm in my right mind or not, but I just thought I heard a baby crying! A new baby, it sounded like—somewhere in this house!"

Little Susan

The Nurse had been looking for hours for the baby she thought she had heard. No one else had heard it. And she had not heard it again. But she kept on looking. She had looked everywhere—everywhere but in the little room up over the kitchen where the Cook slept.

Right now the Cook was snoring loudly in the living room. She had fallen sleep in the easy chair, over her book. No one knew whether or not her glue was dry, for no one had the heart to wake her.

Mr. and Mrs. Doll and the children had been working hard for hours—scrubbing, dusting, shaking out rugs, making beds, washing dishes, and putting things away.

Mrs. Doll had taken down all the curtains, washed them, ironed them, and hung them again. The children had put the nursery in order. Mr. Doll had gathered together a number of odd things that no one seemed to want, and had piled them in the living room on the rug. Most of these things he had never seen before. He did not even know what some of them were. The large wooden egg with the purple pansy painted on it was in the pile. So was the big elastic garter, the big button, and the bright green marble.

"Say, dear—" said Mrs. Doll, coming into the living room for the carpet sweeper, "what are you planning to do with all those things?"

"Well—" said Mr. Doll, "I thought I'd throw all of them away."

"Oh, you had better not do that," said Mrs. Doll. "Very likely they belong to Susan. Why don't you take them to Cook's room? There they'll be out of the way."

Mr. Doll rolled up his sleeves, lifted the large wooden egg, and carried it upstairs. In the bathroom he set it down for a minute, to rest his arms.

"Oh! Mr. Doll! You startled me!" said the Nurse, getting up from the floor in the nursery. She had just been looking under the bed for the baby. "Where are you going with that thing?"

"I'm taking it to Cook's room," said Mr. Doll.

"Cook's room!" said the Nurse. "I forgot all about Cook's room! I'll bet the baby's in there!"

"Now, Nurse!" said Mr. Doll. "How could a baby have got into Cook's room?"

"Now, Mr. Doll!" said the Nurse. "There's a baby *somewhere* in this house! Mark my words!"

Mr. Doll took up the egg again and carried it to the edge of the bathroom, on the open side of the house. Getting it into Cook's room was going to be a dangerous thing for him to do. He would have to step around the wall that separated Cook's room from the rest of the house. Around the wall—on the open side!—was the only way to Cook's room.

"Here—let me help you, Mr. Doll!" said the Nurse, taking one end of the egg.

Together they managed to get it to Cook's room.

And there, on Cook's bed, fastened to a piece of white cardboard, was a brand-new baby, sound asleep. Mr. Doll was so surprised he let go of his end of the egg. The egg rolled across the floor and fell right out of the house. Bang! it went, down below, just outside the kitchen. It made such a noise it woke the baby, and the baby began to cry.

But the Nurse knew just what to do. She unfastened the baby from the cardboard, and took it into her arms. "There, there, little treasure!" she said, rocking it back and forth. Then she said, "See, Mr. Doll? What did I tell you?"

Mrs. Doll, who had been in the kitchen when the egg fell, came running upstairs. She peeked around the wall into Cook's room. "Say, what's going on—Oh! What a *sweet* baby!" she said, reaching out her arms. "Let me take it, Nurse."

"Dear sakes, Mrs. Doll! Don't drop it!" said the Nurse as she handed the baby to her, around the wall. "It's *china*!"

"Is it a boy or a girl, Nurse?" asked Mrs. Doll when she had it safe in her arms.

"I think it must be a girl, Mrs. Doll," said the Nurse, stepping around the wall herself. "See the pink bows on her bonnet? 'Pink for a girl—blue for a boy,' they say. That's what *I've* always heard, anyway."

"I see some pink cheeks, too!" said Mrs. Doll, smiling at the baby.

Mr. Doll came stepping around the wall. He looked at the baby. "Why!" he said, wagging his head. "She's a little beauty!"

"Children!" called Mrs. Doll as she laid the baby on the bed in the nursery.

The children came running.

"Look! You have a new little sister!" said their mother.

"Oh! She's *cute*!" said the children. "Where did you find her?"

"In Cook's room," said the Nurse.

"What was she doing in there?" asked the children.

"Sleeping," said the Nurse, chucking the baby under the chin. "She's as good as gold, *she* is! Aren't you, little treasure?"

"But—where did she come from?" asked the children.

Mrs. Doll sat down on the edge of the bed. "From Susan, of course, my dears," she said. "Your father and I asked Susan for her a long time ago. And now—see? Here she is!"

"Oh! Then, Mother—" said the children. "Susan did *not* forget!"

"Why, *no*, my dears," said their mother. "Susan would never forget. Haven't I always told you that?"

"Yes, Mother—" said the children, "but you thought—you *cried* —you said—"

"I'm sorry I cried, my dears." Mrs. Doll patted them each on the head. "That was no way for a mother to do, was it? Especially this year. Just *see* what Susan has given us *this* year!" she said, smiling at the baby.

"What are we going to call the baby, Mother?" asked the children.

"Well—" said their mother, thinking, "now—let's see. What *could* we call her?"

"We could call her Little Susan!" said the children, right away.

"We could indeed," said their mother. "Why! What a *sweet* idea, my dears!"

No Crib

"I'm sorry to have to say it," said Mr. Doll, turning from the nursery window where he had been looking out, "but—morning is near. This Wonderful Night is almost over, and there won't be another for a whole year."

"Mercy!" said Mrs. Doll. "Is everything finished? Is the house all in order?"

"I have a few odd things, still, to carry to Cook's room," said Mr. Doll. "I must hurry! There isn't much time!"

Down he hurried, to the living room. He tried to pick up all the odd things that were left in the pile. But he could not possibly carry them all. He would have to make several trips. He gathered the big elastic garter into a bunch, and hurried with it up to Cook's room.

In the nursery Mrs. Doll said, "There ought to be a baby's crib somewhere in this house, Nurse. Didn't we used to have one for the other children?"

"There's no crib that *I* know of, Mrs. Doll," said the Nurse.

"Oh, dear!" said Mrs. Doll. "Little Susan must have a bed!"

"A clothes basket would do, Mrs. Doll," said the Nurse. "Have you a clothes basket?"

"Why, yes," said Mrs. Doll. "But I have no idea where it is."

"Well, why don't we look for it?" asked the Nurse.

"Have we time?" asked Mrs. Doll.

"Of course we have!" said the Nurse. "If we hurry!"

"Children, take good care of Little Susan while we're gone!" called Mrs. Doll as she and the Nurse hurried into the bathroom and down the stairs, to look for the clothes basket.

"Hello, Little Susan!" said the children, crowding around the baby and smiling at her.

Little Susan waved her tiny hands and smiled back at them.

"Look!" said George. "She loves us!"

"We love you, too, Little Susan!" said Ann.

"You don't have to sleep in an old clothes basket, Little Susan!" said Tommy.

"You can stay right here, Little Susan!" said the other children. "You can have *our* bed!"

Jane lifted Little Susan in her arms, while the other children opened their bed and puffed up their pillow. When all was ready, Jane laid Little Susan down again; and the other children covered her nicely with their little white quilt. It was rather a stiff little quilt, the kind that sometimes comes in a big box of chocolate candy.

"There you are, Little Susan!" said Mary, patting the quilt. "Now what would you like? Some toys to play with?"

Little Susan waved her tiny hands again.

"You can have *our* toys to play with, Little Susan!" said Freddie. "You can have all our toys!"

The children brought their toys and showed them to Little Susan, one after the other.

"We're sorry they're so old, Little Susan," said Jane. "You see—we didn't get any new toys this year."

"*This* year we got something better—oh! a million times better!" said all the children together. "We got *you*, Little Susan! We got *you*!"

But Little Susan wasn't listening. She was sound asleep.

The children laid the toys around her, on the bed, in case she should wake up and want them. Then they laid themselves down on the floor.

"I'm afraid there's no time left at all, Nurse!" said Mrs. Doll as they hurried upstairs.

They had not found the clothes basket.

"Dear sakes, Mrs. Doll!" said the Nurse when she saw the baby asleep on the bed with all the old toys around her, and the children asleep on the floor. "Look!"

Mrs. Doll looked.

"Did you ever—" laughed the Nurse.

"Sh!" whispered Mrs. Doll, not laughing at all. "Don't waken them! I want Mr. Doll to see them, just as they are. Hurry, Nurse! Tell him to come—quickly!"

The Nurse hurried downstairs, looking for Mr. Doll. She looked into the living room. But only the Cook was there, still snoring loudly. Through the dining room into the kitchen hurried the Nurse. And there she found Mr. Doll, nibbling at the plaster coffee cake.

"Your wife wants you! Quick!" said the Nurse, hurrying back to the living room. She pushed the little button which was glued to the wall, and out went the pretend-light everywhere in the house.

It was no longer needed, for morning was here.

“What’s the matter, dear?” asked Mr. Doll, hurrying upstairs.

“Sh! I just wanted you to see what our children have done!” whispered Mrs. Doll. “Not only have they given Little Susan their bed—they’ve given her all their toys!”

Mr. Doll smiled and put his arm around his little celluloid wife.

The morning light was shining, now, through the nursery window. It shone on the children asleep on the floor. It shone on the baby asleep on the bed. It shone on all the toys. And, somehow or other, the toys did not look old any more. They looked new—brand-new!

Mr. Doll wanted to say something—something he had never been able to say before. But even now he could not say it, for—

The Wonderful Night was over. The light of Christmas Morning came shining in through *all* the windows. And the house was suddenly *very* still.

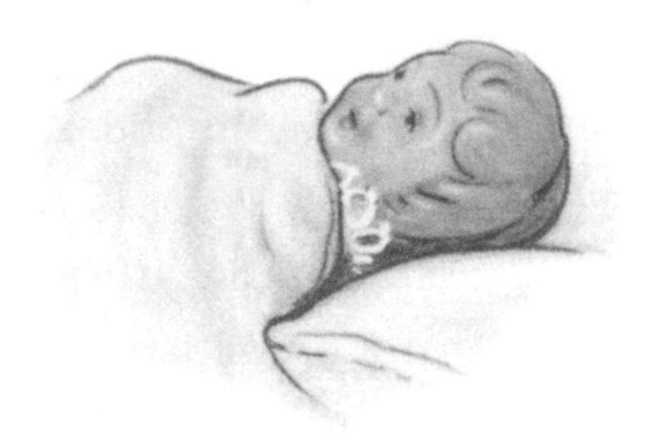

Even Bigger than Susan

Mrs. Doll stood in the nursery, unable to speak or to move, with her husband's arm still around her. She stood looking at all her children as the light of Christmas Morning shone more and more brightly upon them. Her children had always seemed beautiful to her. But now, in this light, they seemed more beautiful than ever before.

Mrs. Doll stood there, half dreaming. And it seemed to her that some Wonderful Person, even bigger than Susan, reached into the house and lifted her out, and undressed her, and then—gently dressed her again, and put her to bed, and covered her nicely, as if she were a little celluloid child. And a sweet, faint smell seemed to be in the air—a smell more like flowers than tooth paste.

Mrs. Doll lay, half dreaming, in her soft, clean bed. She tried to think who this Wonderful Person with hands even gentler than Susan's could be. Then—she fell sound asleep.

And when she awoke she was being lifted out of the house again —*this* time by Susan.

"Why, Mrs. Doll!" said Susan, holding her gently in one hand. "You have a new dress on! What a pretty new dress!"

Mr. Doll was in Susan's other hand. "And just look at your husband in his brand-new suit!" said Susan, holding them so that they could look at each other.

"Mercy!" thought Mrs. Doll. "I'd hardly know him! What a *stunning* suit!"

Indeed it was. It had been cut from a black silk umbrella.

"And just look at all your presents!" said Susan as she set Mr. and Mrs. Doll down, in the living room.

Why! In the middle of the living room rug stood a Christmas tree trimmed with shiny tinsel. And on it, and beneath it, and all around it were more presents than Mr. and Mrs. Doll had ever seen. Some were wrapped in white tissue paper and tied with red string. Some were wrapped in red tissue paper and tied with white string. And to each was fastened a little label with something written on it.

"I'll wake the children, Mrs. Doll," said Susan. "Or—excuse me! —maybe *you* would like to, since it's Christmas Morning."

Susan picked up Mrs. Doll and set her down in the nursery. The six celluloid children were asleep on their bed, and nicely covered!

Mrs. Doll's first thought was "Where is Little Susan?" But she didn't say it out loud. Instead, she kissed the children and they woke up.

"There are lots of surprises, children—" she said, "down in the living room. But, first, let me whisper the nicest surprise of all to you!"

"You have a new little sister!" whispered their mother.

The children stared at her. Why, they knew that! They knew about Little Susan!

Then they caught sight of one of Big Susan's taffy-colored pigtails not far from their bed. And they understood. The Wonderful Night had ended while they had been asleep. It was Big Susan who was speaking for them now. It would be a whole year before they could speak again—for themselves. But that was all right. They didn't mind.

"A little sister!" they shouted, very much surprised, getting out of bed. "Where is she?"

"In here—" said Mrs. Doll, leading the way into the next room, and not quite knowing why, until—

They all saw Little Susan sound asleep in a brand-new crib.

"Oh!" said the children, crowding around the crib. "She has her *own* bed—hasn't she?"

"Of course she has," said Mrs. Doll, leaning over, very stiffly, to pick up Little Susan.

"Let me help you, Mrs. Doll!" said Big Susan. "She's made of china, and she *might* break!"

Big Susan reached in with one hand and picked up Little Susan between two fingers. Then she reached in with both hands and picked up Mrs. Doll and the six children. A moment later they were down in the living room.

"Look at the Christmas tree!" shouted Tommy.

"Look at the presents!" shouted Mary.

"I want a wrist watch!" shouted Freddie.

"Will you *never* be still about that wrist watch, Freddie?" laughed Mr. Doll.

"Who is *this* for?" asked George, meaning a big, bulgy present wrapped in white tissue paper and tied with a red string.

"Let's see!" said Jane, reading the little label that was fastened on it. "It says *For Mrs. Doll.* Mother! It's for you! Open it!"

for the Nurse
for the Baby
For Mr. Doll
For Mrs. Doll
for Freddie

Mrs. Doll laid Little Susan on the sofa while she untied the string. This was rather a difficult thing for celluloid hands to do. Big Susan had to help her. Then Mr. Doll helped her to tear off the tissue paper. And there, inside, was—

a beautiful tea set of shiny gold! There were three cups and saucers, a teapot, a sugar bowl, a cream pitcher, and a tray to stand them on.

"A *luster* tea set!" said Mrs. Doll. "Oh! That's something I've always dreamed of having!"

There was a present wrapped in red tissue paper for Mr. Doll. Inside the tissue paper was a box. And inside the box was a beautiful desk set. There was a fancy inkwell made of gold, with a tiny glass bottle that would hold—one drop of *real* ink! There was a pen made from a toothpick, a writing tablet, some envelopes, and several tiny green stamps.

"Ah ha!" said Mr. Doll. "This is more like it! This is something *I've* always dreamed of having!"

For Jane there was a pair of red bedroom slippers. She put them right on. For George there was a toy train—for Ann, a doll—for Tommy, a tiny birch-bark canoe to sail in the bathtub—for Mary, a toy kitten—for Freddie, a comb.

To the biggest, bulgiest present of all was fastened a little label which said *For the baby*. With Big Susan's help Mr. and Mrs. Doll unwrapped it. It was a white celluloid baby buggy with wheels that *really* turned. Inside it were a tiny quilt made of silk and a tiny pillow made of lace.

"Oh! What a *beautiful* buggy!" said Mrs. Doll, and she laid Little Susan right in it.

Then there was a present that said *For the Cook*, and one that said *For the Nurse*.

"Mercy!" said Mrs. Doll. "Where are *they*?"

All the Presents in the World

With both her hands Big Susan reached into the living room, picked up Mr. and Mrs. Doll and their six children, and, a moment later, set them down in the kitchen.

The Cook was preparing dinner. Her wig was on. Her bandage was gone. And she was her old self again.

"Ach!" she said, wobbling busily about. "What a dinner! What a dinner!"

In a big pot on the stove a *real* Brussels sprout was cooking. Another pot was full of delicious pretend-soup. In the oven was a brand-new plaster turkey, nice and shiny on the outside. On the table were some *real* chocolate puddings, on plates, for dessert.

"Yun! Yum!" said Mr. Doll, staring at the puddings.

"Dinner's almost ready, Mrs. Doll!" said the Nurse, coming in from the dining room. She had just finished setting the table.

"Oh! Look at the table!" said Jane, going into the dining room.

Everyone followed Jane into the dining room, to see the table.

In the center of the table was a basket of *real* cranberries. At each place was a glass of *real* water. Over the table hung a piece of *real* holly, tied with red string to the chandelier.

"How *pretty*!" said Mrs. Doll. "Now, children, hurry and wash your hands! Let Big Susan help you!"

Big Susan picked up the children, one by one, and set them, one by one, in the bathroom.

"Mother!" called Tommy, very much excited. "There's a cake of *real* soap up here!"

"It's pink!" called Ann.

"And, Mother!" called George. "There are *towels*."

"Each towel has a fancy D on it!" called Jane. "In blue!"

"*Mother*!" called Freddie. "There's a *real* sponge in the bathtub!"

"How *nice*!" called Mrs. Doll.

When the children had washed their hands and were down in the dining room again, Mrs. Doll said, "Now let's sit down."

"But there are more presents to open!" said the children. "Lots more!"

"They can wait until after dinner, can't they?" said Mrs. Doll. "Say, dear—would you like to wheel the baby in? Poor little thing, she can't eat the things we eat; but I know she'd like to be here!"

Mr. Doll went into the living room and came back wheeling Little Susan in her brand-new buggy.

Then, very stiffly, the Doll family sat down.

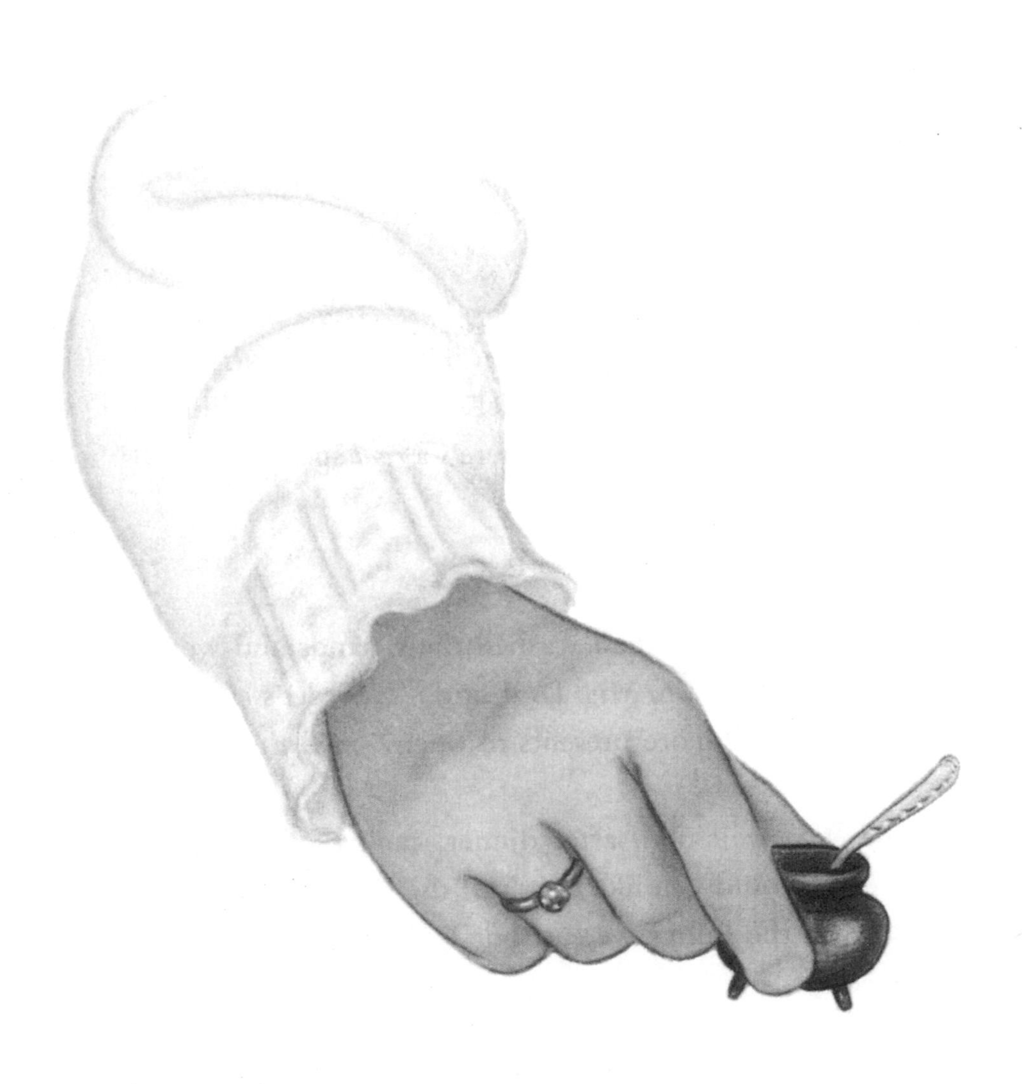

First they had the pretend-soup. Then they had the plaster turkey; the Brussels sprout; and a piece of popcorn on each plate, for mashed potato. There were pieces of puffed rice for rolls, and there was a bowl of green tissue-paper salad. Then came the chocolate puddings and after-dinner coffee. It was pretend-coffee; so the children could have it, too.

"Ah me!" said Mr. Doll, getting up, very stiffly, from the table. "I don't know when I've eaten such big dinner!"

"Cook!" said Mrs. Doll, peeping into the kitchen. "That was a lovely dinner!"

"Thank you kindly, ma'am!" said the Cook. She and the Nurse were sitting at the kitchen table enjoying their share.

"When you finish," said Mrs. Doll, "come into the living room! Just leave the dishes. There are some presents for you in there."

"Presents?... For us?... Ach!... Thank you, Mrs. Doll!" they said.

Then Mrs. Doll wheeled Little Susan back into the living room, where the children were already opening more presents.

For Jane there was a red hair ribbon—for Ann, a blue hair ribbon—for Mary, a yellow hair ribbon—for Tommy, a white candy Life Saver—for George, a toy dog—for Freddie, a wrist watch.

"A wrist watch!" he shouted. It was only a tiny cardboard one, fastened to bit of elastic band. But it made him very happy. "A wrist watch!" he shouted, once more. Then he put it on his wrist, with the help of Big Susan, and was still—at last!

For Mrs. Doll there was a tiny bottle of *real* perfume. For Mr. Doll there was pocket knife that would *really* open and close. For all the children together there was a tiny doll house—with a tiny wooden doll inside it, washing some tiny paper clothes. For Little Susan to play with, there was a white celluloid rattle which was really a collar button.

For the whole family there was a tiny photograph of Big Susan smiling, in a gold frame. Also there was a box of *real* cinnamon candy, and a tiny pack of *real* cards.

After a while the Nurse and the Cook came in, to open *their* presents.

For the Nurse there was a pair of Indian moccasins, made of *real* leather, with tiny beads sewn on the toes. (*...in case you ever have tired feet!* said the little label.)

"Ever! Dear sakes! I *always* have tired feet!" said the Nurse, putting her moccasins right on, with the help of Big Susan. "Well, I declare! They *fit*!"

For the Cook there was a little Chinese pocketbook with a *real* clasp. Inside was a *real* penny.

"Ach!" said the Cook, tucking her pocketbook under her arm. "Ain't *I* the rich lady though!"

Now there were no more presents to open—which was just as well, for things were scattered all over the floor; things were piled upon the sofa, on top of the piano, on the green velvet footstool, and on the seat of the easy chair. The living room was full to overflowing with things. And tissue paper was everywhere.

"Gracious!" laughed Mr. Doll. "It looks as if all the presents in the world had been opened in our living room!"

"Indeed it does!" said Mrs. Doll, laughing too. Then she stopped laughing. "Indeed I think we ought to give thanks for the many, many lovely surprises we have had today. I think we ought to thank Big Susan—right away!"

Thanks

The Dolls stepped to the edge of the living room, at the open side of the house. They stood in a row, with Little Susan in her buggy in the middle.

Big Susan was sitting before the house with her feet tucked under her. The Dolls could see almost all of her from where they stood.

"Big Susan—" Mr. Doll began, looking 'way up at her face, "we thank you for the many, many lovely surprises we have had today. We thank you for our Christmas tree, and for all our presents, and for our big Christmas dinner—"

"Oh, you mustn't thank *me* for those things, Mr. Doll!" said Big Susan. "I was just as surprised as you were!"

"What!" said Mr. Doll. Why, he could hardly believe it!

Mrs. Doll believed it, though. She believed there was someone even bigger than Big Susan—someone whose hands... But she decided to say nothing about it. She said something else instead. "Big Susan—" she said, "there are other things we can thank you for—many other things! We can thank you for all you have ever done for us. We can thank you for your help and for your care. And we can thank you, I'm sure, for someone very small—someone who means more to us than all the presents in the world. We call her Little Susan, you know!"

Big Susan's smile was a wonderful sight to see.

"There's something I'm sure I can thank *you* for, Mrs. Doll!" said Big Susan, smiling. "How *nice* and *clean* the house looks today!"

The End